My Baby Record Book

Illustrated by Paola Bertolini Grudina

Celebrate the miracle of your new baby.
Record those special moments and
make this baby record book
a special keepsake.

In the Beginning

"You have looked deep into my heart,
LORD, and you know all about me.
You notice everything I do; protect me and keep me safe.
You put me together inside my mother's body,
you formed me in my mother's womb.
You know every bone in my body; you know exactly
how I was made.
You watched me grow from conception to birth;
all the stages of my life were spread
out before you, the days of my life
all prepared before I'd even lived
one day.
I praise you because of the
wonderful way you created me.
Lead me in the ways of truth,
dear Lord, and guide me
on the road to eternal life."
Based on Psalm 139

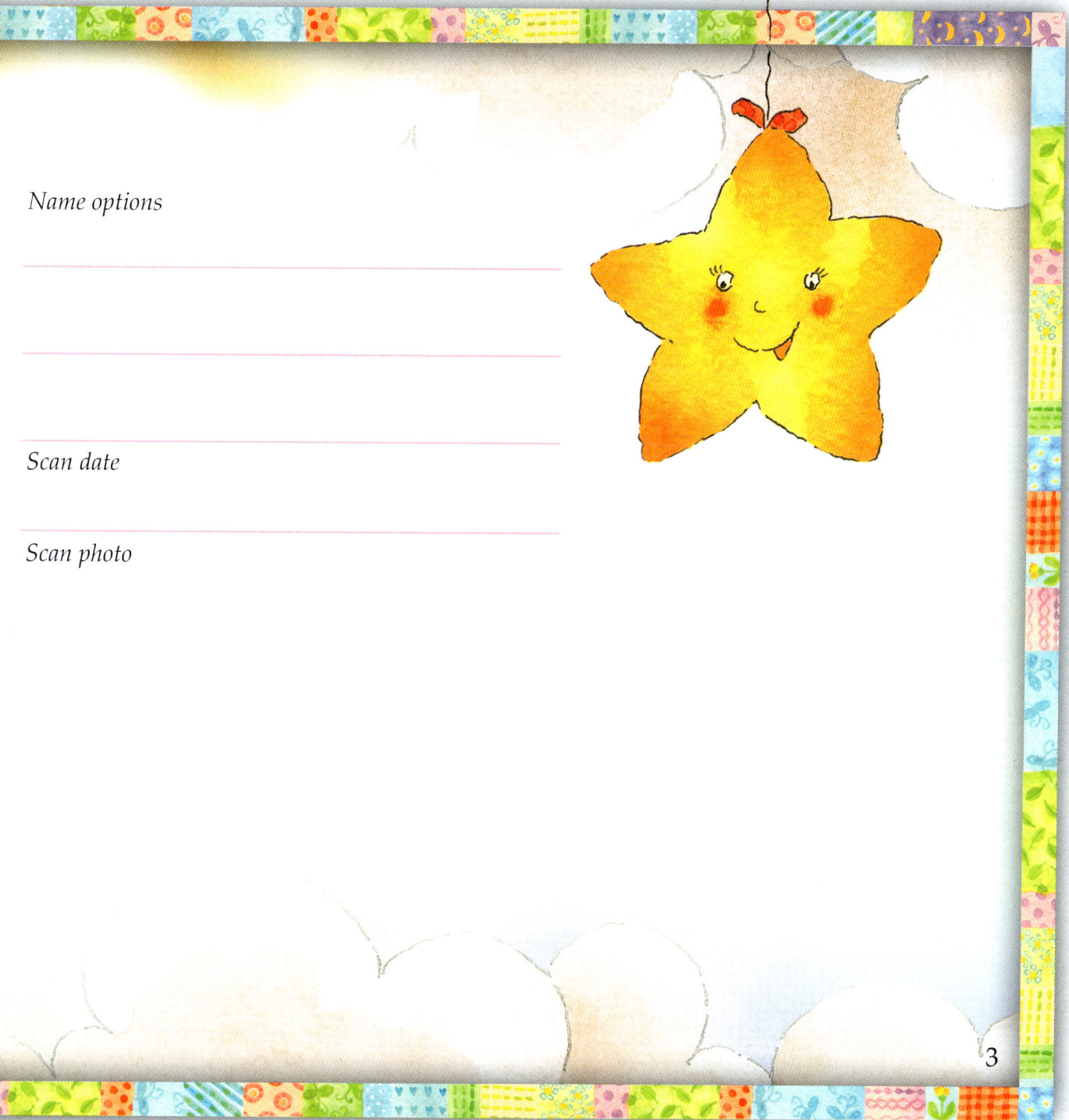

Name options

_____

_____

Scan date

_____

Scan photo

A New Baby

This is my name

_____

This is the date of my birth

_____

I was born at this time

_____

This is the place where I was born

_____

I weighed this much

_____

This is the colour of my hair

_____

This is the colour of my eyes

_____

Children are a blessing and a gift from the Lord.

Psalm 127:3

Father God, maker of all that is good,
this new baby fills us with wonder and awe.
Thank you for giving us this precious new life
to protect and nurture.
Help us through all the joys and struggles ahead
to love and care for our new baby,
this special gift from you.

My First Visitors

Thank you, Father God,
for the safe delivery of this new baby,
for the miracle of new life,
for the wonder of a new creation,
and for the mystery of human love.
Thank you that you know our names
and you have loved us from the very beginning.
Be near us as we learn the joys and challenges of being parents,
and help us to trust you to provide for all our needs.

The people who came to see me

My Family

Name
_____

Date and place of birth
_____

Name
_____

Date and place of birth
_____

Name
_____

Date and place of birth
_____

Name
_____

Date and place of birth
_____

Name
_____

Date and place of birth
_____

Thank you, Lord, for brothers and sisters,
aunties and uncles and cousins.
Thank you for the gift of my family.
Thank you that you are here with us,
that your love surrounds us,
and that you have given us each other to care for,
learn from and share with, day by day.

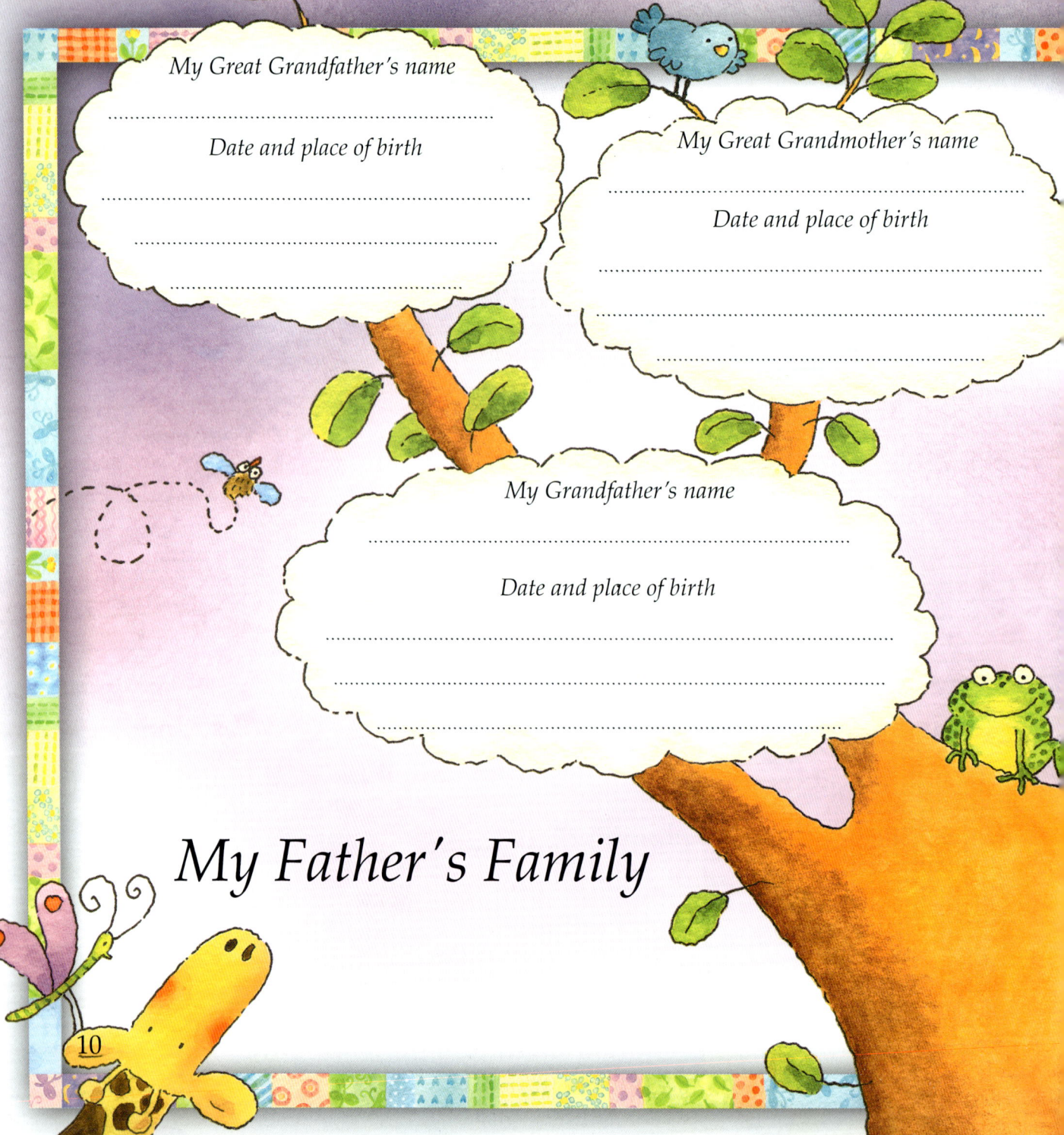

My Great Grandfather's name

....

Date and place of birth

....

....

....

My Great Grandmother's name

....

Date and place of birth

....

....

....

My Grandfather's name

....

Date and place of birth

....

....

....

My Father's Family

My Great Grandmother's name

....

Date and place of birth

....

....

My Great Grandfather's name

....

Date and place of birth

....

....

....

My Grandmother's name

....

Date and place of birth

....

....

....

My Father's name

....

Date and place of birth

....

....

11

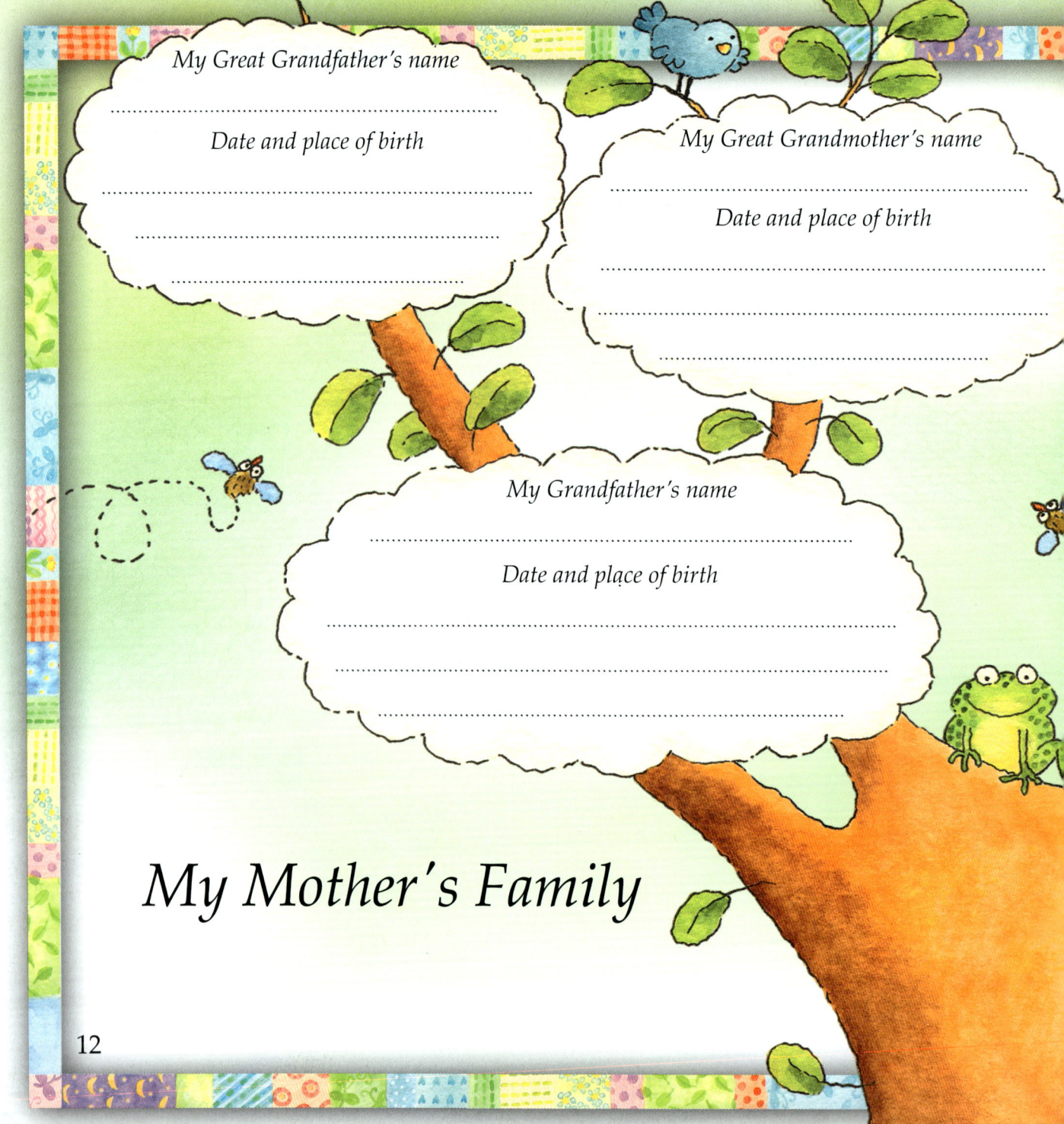

My Great Grandfather's name

....

Date and place of birth

....

....

....

My Great Grandmother's name

....

Date and place of birth

....

....

....

My Grandfather's name

....

Date and place of birth

....

....

....

My Mother's Family

My Great Grandmother's name

....

Date and place of birth

....

....

....

My Great Grandfather's name

....

Date and place of birth

....

....

....

My Grandmother's name

....

Date and place of birth

....

....

....

My Mother's name

....

Date and place of birth

....

....

....

13

My Grandparents

Father God,
Thank you for giving us families to care for us.
Thank you for those who have been anxious
as we have been anxious;
for those who have been strong when problems arise.
Thank you for their wisdom and courage and strength.
Help us to learn from those who have gone before us
And love them as they love us.

Things my grandparents wish for me

_____

_____

_____

_____

Things my grandparents want me to know about

them

_____

_____

_____

_____

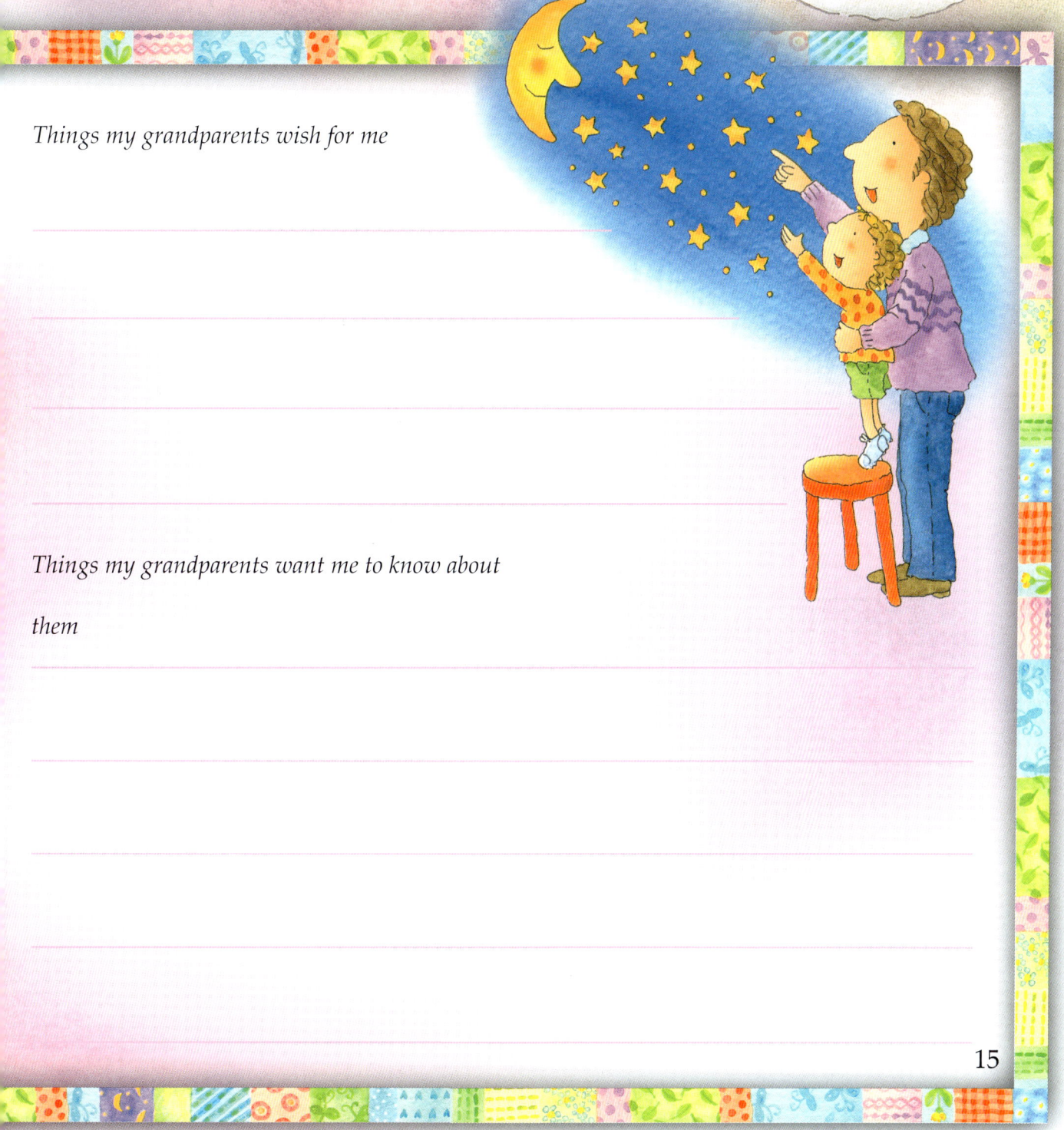

My Home

My home address

_____

_____

_____

Lord Jesus, you shared in Nazareth the life of an earthly home.
Bless our home now with peace and joy.
Give to parents strength and wisdom
as the sun rises each morning,
Love and patience to get through each day,
and peaceful rest as the stars light up the night sky.

Lord God,
You made the world and it was very good.
Lord God,
You gave me a home,
a place where I can be safe from harm.
Lord God,
You gave me people to love me and care for me.
Thank you for all the good things you have given me.

What my room looks like

My Progress

Date of my first smile

_____

Date of my first tooth

_____

I first slept through the night on

_____

Lord, bless us and protect us.
Lord, smile on us and show us your love.
Lord, take care of us and help us.

19

My Special Things

My pets

My best friends

My favourite toys

My favourite story

My favourite game

My favourite sound

My favourite colour

My favourite foods

My favourite drinks

Things I like to do

Dear God,
Thank you for my friends.
Thank you for my toys and special things.
Please teach me to share all I have with others.
Amen

Thank you for the world so sweet,
Thank you for the food we eat,
Thank you for the birds that sing,
Thank you God for everything.

Special Times

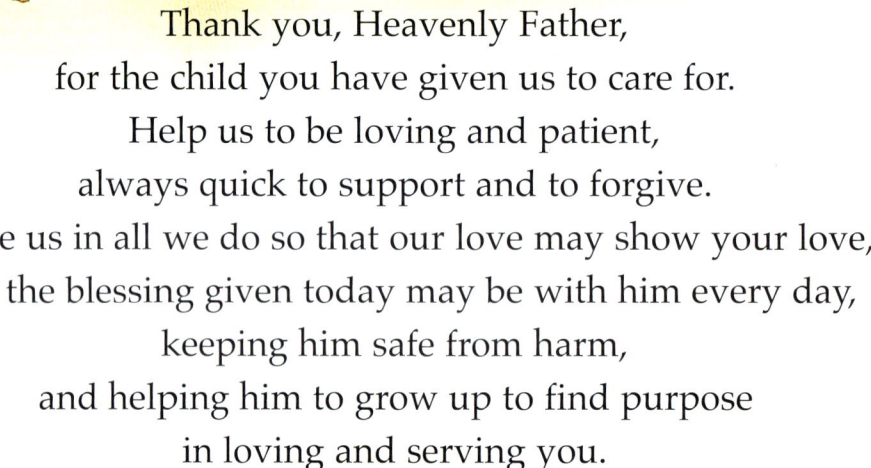

Thank you, Heavenly Father,
for the child you have given us to care for.
Help us to be loving and patient,
always quick to support and to forgive.
Guide us in all we do so that our love may show your love,
and the blessing given today may be with him every day,
keeping him safe from harm,
and helping him to grow up to find purpose
in loving and serving you.

Date of baptism

Age at baptism

Place of baptism

Names of godparents or sponsors

Who came

I spent my first Christmas at
_____

I shared my first Christmas with
_____

On my first Christmas I ate
_____

The church I attended on my first Christmas was
_____

I spent my First Easter at
_____

I shared my First Easter with
_____

On my First Easter I ate
_____

The Church I attended on my First Easter was
_____

Where I spent my first holiday
_____

Special places I saw and visited
_____

The people I shared my first holiday with
_____

Things I did on my first holiday
_____

Publishing Director: Annette Reynolds
Art Director: Gerald Rogers
Pre-production Manager: Doug Hewitt

Printed and bound in China

Baby's First Prayers

Illustrated by Paola Bertolini Grudina

*Children are a blessing
and a gift from the Lord.*

Psalm 127:3

God is great!

O Lord God, how great you are!
When I look at the sky,
And the moon and the stars,
I feel so tiny,
I don't understand why you care about me.
O Lord God, how great you are!

Adapted from Psalm 8

Praise God, from whom all blessings flow;
Praise Him, all creatures here below;
Praise Him above, you heavenly host;
Praise Father, Son, and Holy Ghost.

Bishop Thomas Ken

Lord God,
You are great and wonderful
and you made the whole wide world!
You are kind and good,
marvellous and mighty,
ever living, ever loving,
everlasting, everywhere.

Come, bow down and worship him.
Kneel before the Lord, the Creator.
For he is our God, and we are his people.
He loves us and takes care of us.
From Psalm 95

3

Thank you, God

Butterflies thank you for wings to fly,
fish give thanks for the sea.
Birds give thanks with the songs they sing,
but I thank you for making me me!

Bethan James

For this new morning and its light,
For rest and shelter of the night,
For health and food, for love and friends,
For every gift your goodness sends,
We thank you, gracious Lord. Amen.

Traditional

Thank you, God, for making me ME.
Thank you for eyes that see your world,
for ears that hear the things you have made,
a nose so I can smell my dinner cooking
and a mouth to praise you!
Thank you for fingers and toes
and for loving me, just the way I am.
In the name of the Father, and of the Son,
and of the Holy Spirit.
Amen

Sorry

Our Father in heaven,
hallowed be your name.
Your Kingdom come,
your will be done,
on earth as in heaven.
Give us today our daily bread.
Forgive us our sins,
as we forgive those who sin against us.
Lead us not into temptation,
but deliver us from evil.
For the kingdom, the power
and the glory are yours.
Now and for ever. Amen

Based on Matthew 6:10-14

I want to be generous, Lord,
but sometimes it's hard to share.
I want to be kind, Lord,
but sometimes I am mean.
I want to say the right thing,
but sometimes the wrong thing comes out.
I need your help, Lord,
to be generous and kind and loving.
Please help me.

Based on Romans 7:19

Family and friends

Bless our home, dear Lord.
Teach us to love one another,
Support and help one another,
And forgive one another,
As you forgive us.

Sally Ann Wright

Thank you for my friends, Lord.
Thank you for time to play together.
Thank you for storytime and books to look at.
Help me to be ready to share
and ready to say sorry
if things go wrong.

Please God, look after everyone in my family.
Whether at home or far away,
Keep them safe and well today.

Bethan James

Thank you, Father God, for families:
For mums and dads, brothers, sisters,
cousins, aunts, uncles and grandparents.
Help us to love and care for each other
and to be especially kind to each one, today.
Sally Ann Wright

Day by day

Most merciful redeemer,
Friend and brother,
May we know you more clearly,
Love you more dearly,
And follow you more nearly,
Day by day.

Adapted from Richard of Chichester (1253)

Help me to do the things I should,
to be to others kind and good;
in all I do, in work or play,
to grow more loving every day.

10

Christ be with me, Christ within me,
Christ behind me, Christ before me,
Christ beside me, Christ to win me,
Christ to comfort and restore me,
Christ beneath me, Christ above me,
Christ in quiet, Christ in danger,
Christ in hearts of all that love me,
Christ in mouth of friend and stranger.

St Patrick's Breastplate

11

The world around us

Thank you for the world so sweet,
Thank you for the food we eat,
Thank you for the birds that sing,
Thank you, God, for everything. Amen.
Edith Rutter Leatham

Splashy sea,
Big blue sky,
Shiny stones,
Grasses tall.
Trickling sand,
Knobbly shells...
Thank you, God!
You made it all.
Sally Ann Wright

12

Thank you, God,
for making giraffes tall,
and hamsters small,
and ladybirds crawl,
and creatures all
around us!

Bethan James

Spotty ladybirds, stripy snails,
Tiny spiders, buzzing bees,
Slimy slugs with silvery trails,
Wiggly worms and centipedes,
Crawling creatures with long tails:
Thank you, God, you made all
these.

Bethan James

13

Prayers for others

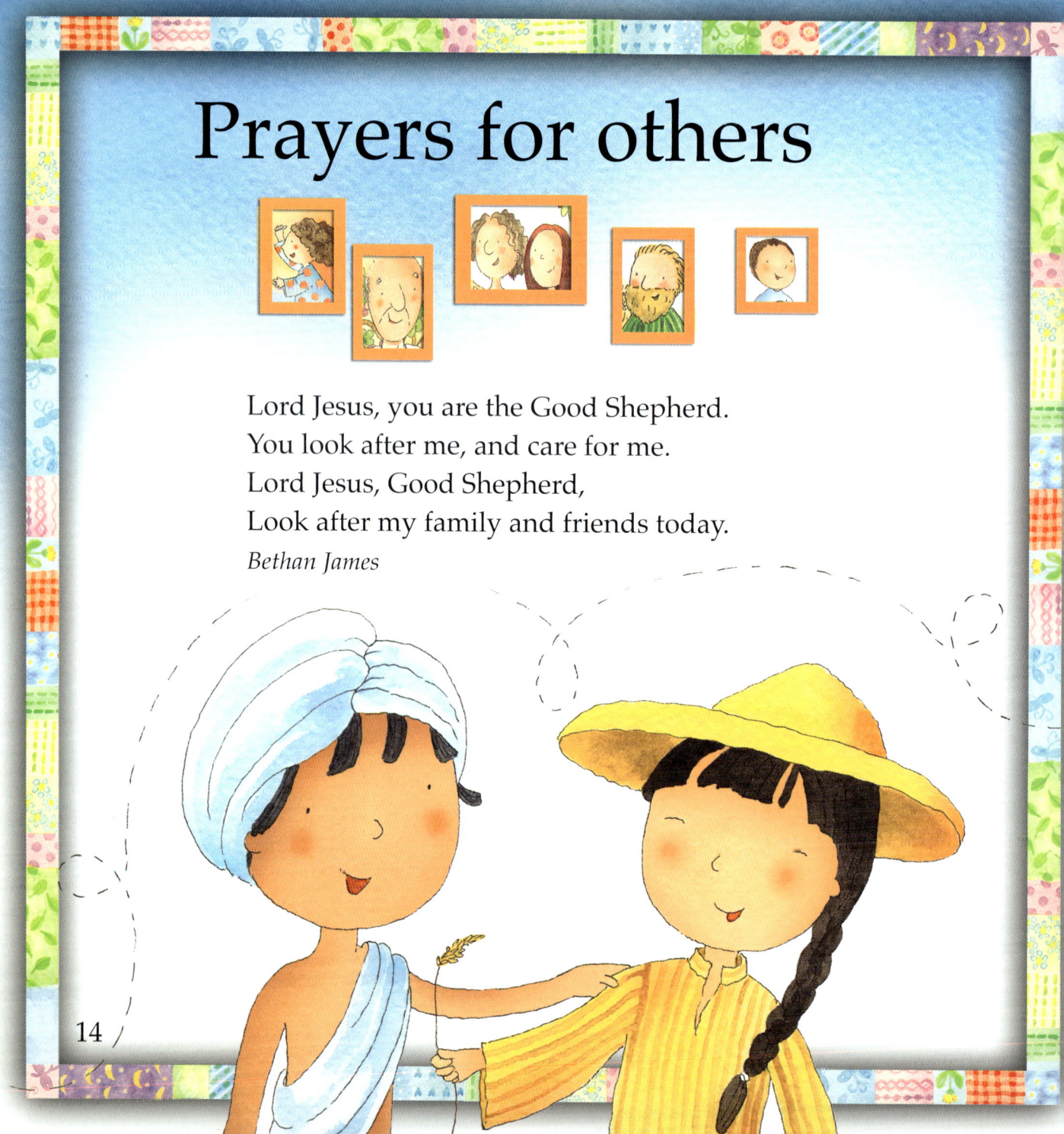

Lord Jesus, you are the Good Shepherd.
You look after me, and care for me.
Lord Jesus, Good Shepherd,
Look after my family and friends today.
Bethan James

14

Loving Father, creator of all people,
you love everyone you have made:
different ages and different sizes,
different shapes and different colours.
Help us to learn from one another,
Share with one another, and love one another.
Bethan James

15

Graces

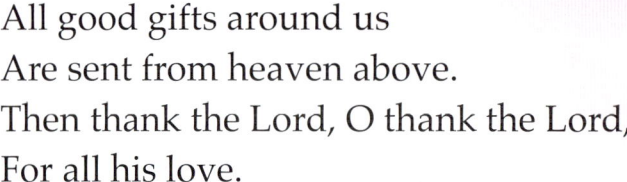

All good gifts around us
Are sent from heaven above.
Then thank the Lord, O thank the Lord,
For all his love.
Matthias Claudius

O God, your generous love surrounds us,
and everything we enjoy comes from you.
The Methodist Service Book

Yours Lord, are the greatness, the power,
the glory and the majesty,
for everything we have comes from you.
Based on 1 Chronicles 29:11

For this and all his many mercies,
God's holy name be blessed
and praised;
through Christ our Lord.
Traditional

16

May the Lord who feeds the little bird,
Bless our food now, we pray.

A prayer from Norway

For every cup and plateful
Lord, make us truly grateful.

Traditional

The eagles give thanks for the mountains,
The fish give thanks for the sea,
We give thanks for our blessings
And for what we're about to receive.

A native American prayer

God is great and God is Good,
And we thank God for our food;
By God's hand we must be fed,
Give us Lord, our daily bread.

Traditional

17

Special times

Dear God, you clothe the lilies of the field,
and feed the birds of the sky.
You lead lambs to pasture and guide deer to water.
Thank you for this special day,
and for all the good gifts you give to us.

18

May the joy of the angels,
the wonder of the shepherds,
and the peace of Jesus Christ,
fill our hearts this
Christmas time.

19

Prayers at bedtime

Jesus, Friend of little children, be a friend to me;
take my hand, and ever keep me close to thee.
Walter J. Matham

Angels bless and angels keep,
Angels guard me while I sleep.
Bless my heart and bless my home,
Bless my spirit as I roam.
Guide and guard me through the night
and wake me with the morning's light.
Traditional

Now I lay me down to sleep,
I pray the Lord my soul to keep.
May God guard me through the night
and wake me with the morning light.

Into your loving care,
Into your keeping,
You who are everywhere,
Take us, we pray.
Traditional

21

Blessings

At the first light of sun:
God bless you.
When the long day is done:
God bless you.
In your smiles and in your tears:
God bless you.
Through each day of your years:
God bless you.

Adapted from an Irish blessing

Lord, bless us
and protect us.
Lord, smile on us and
show us your love
Take care of us and
help us.
Amen

May the Lord bless us and watch over us.
May the Lord make his face shine upon us
and be gracious to us,
may the Lord look kindly on us
and give us peace;
and the blessing of God almighty,
the Father, the Son, and the Holy Spirit,
be with us and remain with us now and
every day.

Based on Numbers 6:24-26

God bless all those that I love;
God bless all those that love me;
God bless all those that love those that I love
And all those that love those that love me.

from a New England sampler

Baby's Bible Stories

Bethan James

Illustrated by Paola Bertolini Grudina

*Special stories to introduce your baby
to the God who made us and all the world.*

God made the world

Long ago, at the beginning of time, there was nothing, nothing but God. God made light to shine in the darkness and he saw that it was good. God shaped the land with hills and mountains surrounded by deep water and filled it with trees and flowering plants. God placed the sun, moon and stars in the sky above.

God filled the waters with fish and the sky with every kind of winged creature. God filled the land with all kinds of animals and made people to look after his beautiful world.

When God saw that his world was very good, he rested from the work of creation.

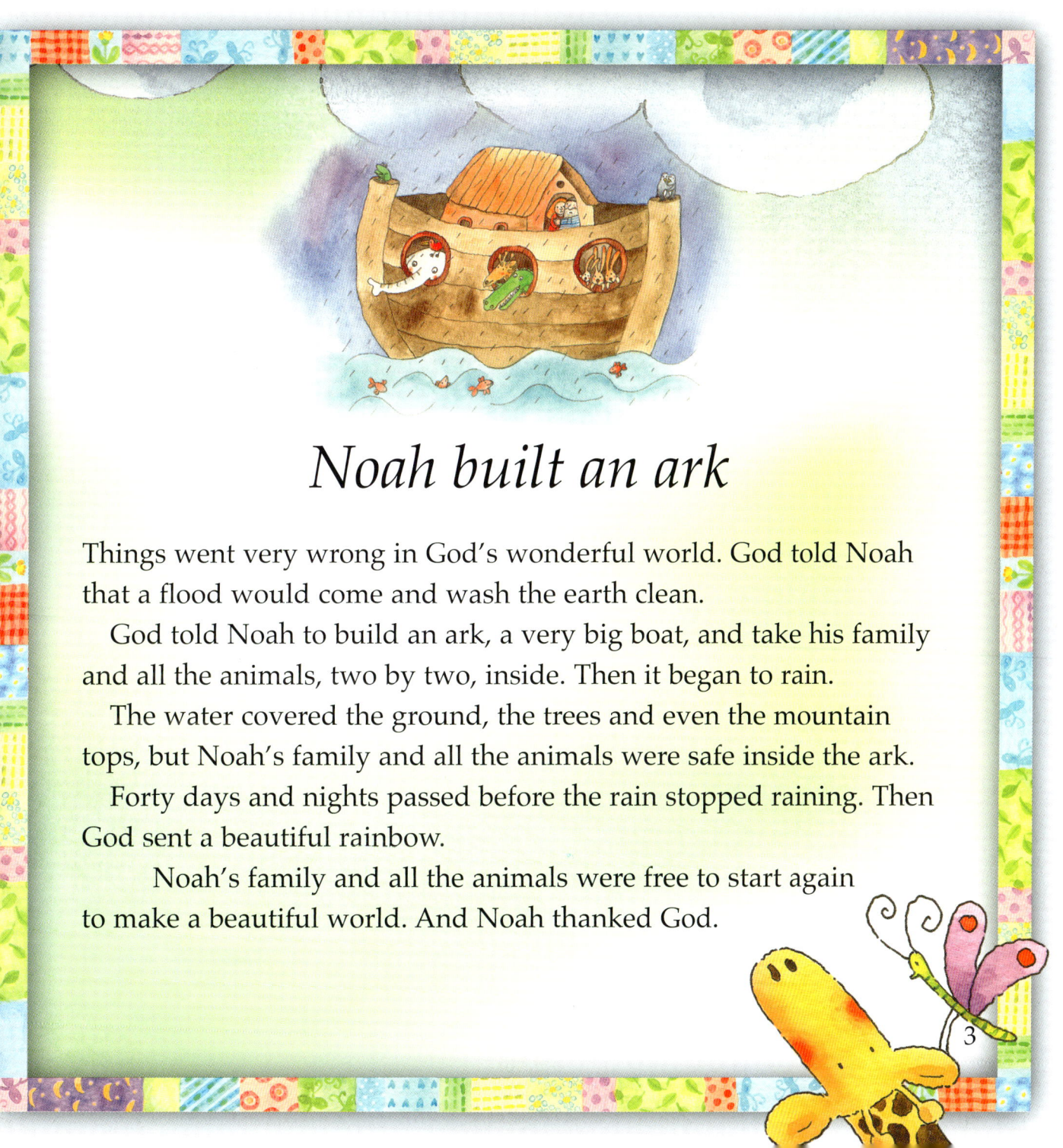

Noah built an ark

Things went very wrong in God's wonderful world. God told Noah that a flood would come and wash the earth clean.

God told Noah to build an ark, a very big boat, and take his family and all the animals, two by two, inside. Then it began to rain.

The water covered the ground, the trees and even the mountain tops, but Noah's family and all the animals were safe inside the ark.

Forty days and nights passed before the rain stopped raining. Then God sent a beautiful rainbow.

Noah's family and all the animals were free to start again to make a beautiful world. And Noah thanked God.

3

The baby in the basket

Baby Moses was crying - loudly.

His mother was so afraid that the king's soldiers would hear him that she wove some reeds into a basket and floated it on the River Nile with baby Moses inside.

The king wanted to kill all the baby boys so they would not grow into men who might fight him.

Big sister Miriam hid in the reeds and watched. And who should come along but the king's own daughter!

'Oh!' said the princess. 'What a sweet baby. I'll look after you!'

Miriam fetched her mother to help so Moses was safe from the soldiers and her mother could still take care of him.

The best way to live

'I am the living God,' God said. 'Don't worship anyone else.

'Don't worship pictures or statues of me.

'Treat my name with respect.

'Rest on the seventh day of the week – make it a happy, holy day, when everyone can worship me together.

'Look after your mums and dads and love them.

'Don't hurt anyone; don't even think about hurting them.

'Don't steal someone else's wife or husband.

'Don't steal anything that belongs to someone else.

'Don't tell lies or say nasty things about other people.

'Don't look at what others have and be unhappy because you don't have them.'

'Love God and be kind to each other,' said a grown up Moses, 'and you will be happy.'

God chooses a king

When the people wanted a good king, Samuel asked God to help him choose the right person.

Jesse brought seven of his sons to Samuel.

'Should it be the tallest and strongest?' thought Samuel. All of them were tall and strong.

'Not the tallest, not the strongest, but the person who is good and true inside,' said God.

'Have you any other sons?' he asked Jesse.

'Well, there's David,' said Jesse. 'But he's out in the fields taking care of my sheep.'

'I'll wait,' said Samuel.

When David came, Samuel said, 'This is the boy God has chosen to be king. Not the tallest, not the strongest, but the person who is good and true inside.'

Elijah and the ravens

'There will be no rain for a very long time,' said Elijah to King Ahab. 'God is not happy with the bad things you are doing.'

God told Elijah to go to a stream for clean water. Every day God sent ravens with food in their beaks. When Elijah's little stream dried up God sent him to the village of Zarephath.

'A widow there will share her food with you.'

'This is all I have,' the widow told Elijah.

But for as long as she shared her food with Elijah, God made sure she had enough flour and oil to make a little more.

Jonah runs the other way

When God told Jonah to go to Nineveh with a message for the cruel people there, Jonah sailed away in the opposite direction.

A big storm blew, and the sailors were afraid they'd be drowned.

'Throw me into the sea!' said Jonah. 'It's all my fault! I've disobeyed God.'

Jonah was swallowed by a very big fish and stayed there for three days and three nights. Jonah told God he was sorry.

Then the very big fish spat Jonah out on to the beach. Jonah went to Nineveh and told the people there to stop doing bad things – and the people said they were sorry!

'That's why I sent you,' said God. 'Now I can forgive these people and we can be friends.'

8

Plots and plans and lions

Daniel was good and wise and loved God. But some bad men plotted and planned and went to the king.

'Anyone who thinks you're not the most special person on earth, oh King, shall be thrown to the lions,' they said.

The king thought it was a good idea. He made it law.

Daniel was good and wise and loved God and he prayed to God, just as he had before.

The king knew that he had to throw Daniel to the lions.

It was a long night for the king, but in the morning the king found Daniel... alive and well!

'I trusted God and he took care of me,' said Daniel.

'Daniel's God is the true and living God,' said the king. 'He is amazing.'

9

A long way to Bethlehem

Mary was going to have a baby – God's baby, the baby Jesus. Joseph married Mary and took care of her. The baby grew inside Mary and soon the time came for her little son to be born.

But the Romans wanted to count all the people in the empire. Mary and Joseph had to travel a long way to Bethlehem.

'No room here!' they were told, when they looked for somewhere to stay. 'But… you can rest in the stable, if you like.'

That night, Mary's baby was born, Jesus, the Son of God. Mary wrapped him up warmly and made a bed for him in the manger where the animals fed.

Following the star

There was a very bright star shining in the sky on the night Jesus was born. Wise men in the East saw the star and wondered what it might mean.

'A new king has been born to the Jewish people,' said one.

'We must take gifts fit for a king,' said another.

'We must go to worship him,' said a third.

They made a long, long journey, following the bright star all the way until they found the new-born king.

They knelt down in wonder and gave him their gifts of gold, frankincense and myrrh. Then they worshipped Jesus, the Son of God.

Talking to God

When Jesus was a man, he loved to talk to God. So he showed his friends how to talk to God too.

'Don't use long words,' Jesus said. 'Tell God what you really feel. He wants to hear about everything that worries you.

'Say something like this: Our Father in heaven, your name is great and holy. Help us to do things that are right so that everyone will know who you are and your love will spread all over the world.

'Please give us enough to eat each day and help us to be kind to each other always. Keep us safe from danger and help us not to do wrong things.

'For you, Lord, are the only true, wise and wonderful God and your kingdom will last for ever.'

God cares about you

Jesus had twelve special friends, disciples who listened to him when he talked about God, his father.

'Don't worry too much about food and clothes,' said Jesus. 'Look at the birds and the flowers. Our Father God looks after the birds and they all find enough to eat. And the wild flowers are beautiful!

'God gives us all we need when we love and trust him and share with each other.'

'God cares for everyone, even the tiniest sparrows,' said Jesus. 'God is great and mighty but he knows if one falls to the ground. He knows us and cares about us too. We are safe in his strong, kind hands.'

The hole in the roof

Jesus didn't just talk about God, he showed people that God cared about them.

One day he was talking to people in a house in Capernaum when dust started falling down into the room. Above him four men were making a hole in the roof! They lowered their friend down through the hole. The man couldn't walk.

'Hello,' said Jesus, smiling. 'You can get up and go home now. Your sins are forgiven and your body is healed.'

The religious teachers muttered at this. Surely only God could forgive sins. But Jesus was God's Son. Everyone was amazed when the man picked up his mat and went home, a new man.

The storm at sea

At the end of a long, tiring day, Jesus and his friends sailed across Lake Galilee. Jesus soon fell asleep.

Suddenly, the wind whistled and the thunder boomed. Waves washed into the boat which lurched up and down. Jesus' friends were very afraid they would drown.

'Wake up!' they said to Jesus. 'Please, help us!'

Jesus stood up and spoke to the wind and waves.

'Hush... be quiet,' said Jesus. And the wind dropped and the waves stopped crashing into the boat. Jesus had calmed a storm. The wind and the waves did just what he said.

Jesus' friends were not afraid of the storm any more. But they looked at Jesus with wonder.

The boy who shared

Thousands of people were listening to Jesus tell them stories about God as if he really knew what God was like. They saw Jesus make blind people see; they saw him make deaf people hear.

But by evening everyone was hungry. Where could they find food for so many people?

Andrew, one of the disciples brought a boy to Jesus. He had five little bread rolls and two little fish he was willing to share.

'Thank you, God, for all you give us,' said Jesus.

The disciples shared out the food with the people around them. Somehow everyone had enough to eat. There were even twelve baskets of food left over! It was a miracle.

The story of the good Samaritan

'How can I show God that I love him?' a man asked Jesus.

'Love God. Look after other people as if you love them too,' Jesus replied. 'Listen: there was once a man who was attacked and robbed and lay beside the road hurting all over. A man passed by but did not stop to help him. Later another man passed by but he didn't stop to help either.

'Then the injured man heard the sound of a donkey's hooves. A man from another country stopped and bathed his wounds, helped him on to the donkey and took him to an inn to get better.

'If you want to show God you love him, be like the stranger, the good Samaritan.'

The story of the lost sheep

'God loves you like a good shepherd loves his sheep!' Jesus once said. Then he told a story.

'Once there was a shepherd who had 100 sheep. But when he counted them safely into their pen, he saw that one was missing.

'The shepherd left his other sheep and clambered over the hillside, over the rocks, looking behind bushes and trees until at last he found his sheep who was lost and alone and frightened.

'Then the shepherd carried the sheep safely in his arms down the steep rocky path. He was so happy to have found his little lost sheep that he called his friends together to have a party.

18   'That's how much God loves you,' said Jesus.

The man who climbed the tree

Zacchaeus wanted very much to meet Jesus. Zacchaeus was a rich tax collector and he didn't have any friends.

Lots of other people wanted to meet Jesus too – and Zacchaeus was too short to see over their heads. So he climbed into the branches of a fig tree.

Jesus saw Zacchaeus in the tree. 'Come down,' said Jesus. 'I'd like to come to your house today.'

The people with Jesus knew Zacchaeus was a cheat. They were surprised at what happened now Jesus was his friend.

'I'll give money back to anyone I have cheated, and share what I have left with the poor,' he said.

'This is why I am here,' said Jesus, 'to help people like Zacchaeus.'

Judas betrays his friend

Jesus had many friends. But he also had enemies, men who did not understand that he was God's son, men who were jealous because he was so popular. Those men had plotted to have Jesus arrested and killed. They had bribed Judas, one of his disciples to betray him.

Jesus and his friends had eaten together in Jerusalem. Jesus offered them bread and said it was like his broken body; he offered them wine and said it was like his blood.

After supper, they went to a garden of olive trees and Jesus asked God to help him to be brave. He knew that Judas was coming with his enemies to arrest him.

Three crosses on a hillside

Jesus was arrested and taken for questioning. They knew he had done nothing wrong. But his enemies wanted him dead.

Then Jesus, the man who had healed people, helped them and been kind to them, who had told them how much God loved them, was crucified on a hillside between two thieves.

Jesus asked God to forgive the soldiers and the thieves and everyone in the world for everything they'd ever done wrong. Jesus was dying for them.

On that Friday afternoon Jesus took his last breath and died.

That evening friends came and took him down from the cross. They buried him in a rock tomb and sealed the opening with a heavy stone door.

Jesus is alive!

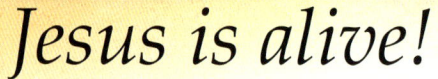

Early on Sunday morning, some of the women who had been his friends took spices to the garden where Jesus was buried. But they found that the stone door had been rolled away. The tomb was empty.

Two angels sat beside the cave.

'Jesus isn't here,' said the angel. 'He is not dead any more – he is alive!' The women ran to tell Jesus' other friends what had happened but Mary Magdalene stayed by the empty cave, crying.

'Mary!' said a kind voice behind her.

Mary knew that voice. It was Jesus! He was alive! She ran back to tell everyone that she had seen him for herself.

Breakfast by the lake

All the disciples except Judas saw Jesus after that. They talked with him and ate with him.

They had been fishing on Lake Galilee one night when they saw him again. Just as the sun was rising, they heard a voice from the water's edge.

'Have you caught anything?' called the man.

'Nothing,' they replied gloomily.

'Put out your net on the other side,' the man shouted back.

Their net became so full of fish that they could hardly pull it in! They knew the man was Jesus. They all ate fish and bread together on the beach.

Jesus went back to be with God. But he left them the Holy Spirit to help them for ever afterwards. The Holy Spirit gave them power to tell the world all about Jesus.

23

This UK edition Copyright © 2018

Sarah Grace Publishing

an imprint of Malcolm Down Publishing

www.malcolmdown.co.uk

First edition 2017

Copyright © 2017 Anno Domini Publishing

www.ad-publishing.com

Text copyright © Bethan James

Illustrations copyright © 2017 Paola Bertolini Grudina

Publishing Director: Annette Reynolds

Art Director: Gerald Rogers

Pre-production Manager: Doug Hewitt

Printed and bound in China